Check out these other exciting STECK-VAUGHN Science Fiction Titles!

How far would you go to break into
the movies? Get the answer in
BEHIND THE SCREAMS

Here today . . . gone tomorrow!
Find out more in
WARP WORLD 3030

It's alive. It's growing. It's *hungry*. See why in
BZZZZ

Earth is in for a big jolt. Check out why in
SHORT CIRCUIT

There's a whole lot of shakin' going on!
Read all about it in
SUPER STAR

All that glitters isn't good! See why in
CHARMERS

History can really get to you! Learn more in
BLAST FROM THE PAST

You may get more than you bargained for!
Check out
COSMIC EXCHANGE

This fan is out of this world!
Find out why in
ALIEN OBSESSION

ISBN 0-8114-9325-3

7 8 9 10 06 05 04

Produced by Mega-Books of New York, Inc.
Design and Art Direction by Michaelis/Carpelis Design Assoc.

Cover illustration: Wayne Alfano

THE LOST LANGUAGE

by Tracey West

interior illustrations by
Frank Mayo

STECK-VAUGHN
COMPANY

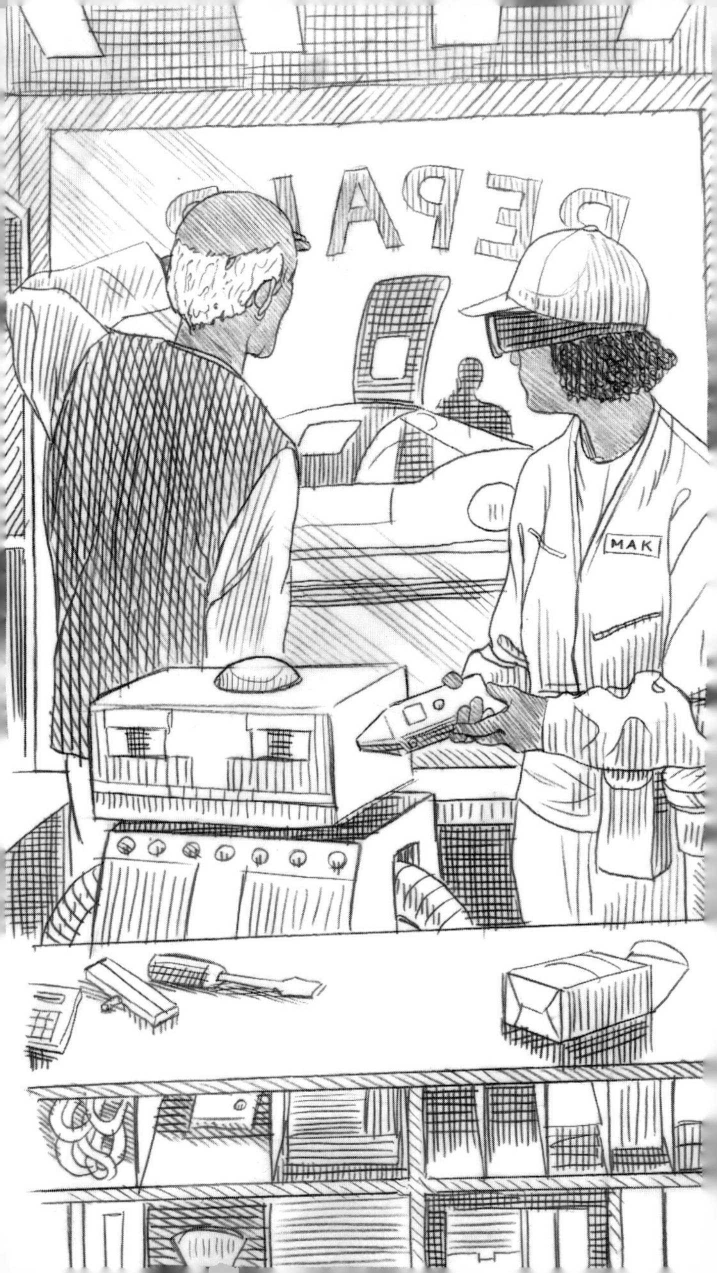
MAK

CHAPTER 1

"We've got a customer."

Mak looked up from the robot she was working on. Her Uncle Paul leaned against the window of their repair shop, shielding his eyes from the desert sun.

Mak took off her safety goggles and walked toward him.

"He's in a four-seater hovercar in pretty good shape," Uncle Paul said. "He must be from New Earth City."

Mak watched as the hovercar floated in midair for a second, then gently sank to the ground outside.

The passenger door opened and a short man stepped out. From the driver's side came a robot. It followed the man to the shop.

"Looks like an AP-15, made around the year 2079," Mak said.

Mak's seventy year-old great-uncle didn't move to greet the man.

Mak opened the door. "May I help you?" she asked.

"Please, miss," the man said. "Is Paul Martinson here?"

"Come on in," said Uncle Paul.

The robot followed the man in. The man stared at the hundreds of spare robot parts that littered the tiny repair shop. There was nothing unusual about the parts to Mak. She'd been staring at them for ten years.

"My name's Ivan Stanley. And this," said the man, pointing to the robot, "is Buffy."

Mak couldn't help laughing.

Mr. Stanley stiffened. "Buffy is nothing to laugh at, miss. She's one of the finest units around. I'll have you know, she's an—"

"All-purpose unit, AP-15. Built in

2079. Right?" Mak said matter-of-factly.

"Why, yes," said Mr. Stanley. "She's only ten years old. She should be in perfect shape. But lately, she's not herself. However, I'm sure it's something very minor."

"If she's been malfunctioning, why did you let her drive the hovercar?" Mak asked.

Mr. Stanley gazed down at the floor. "Well, actually . . . I don't know how to drive a hovercar."

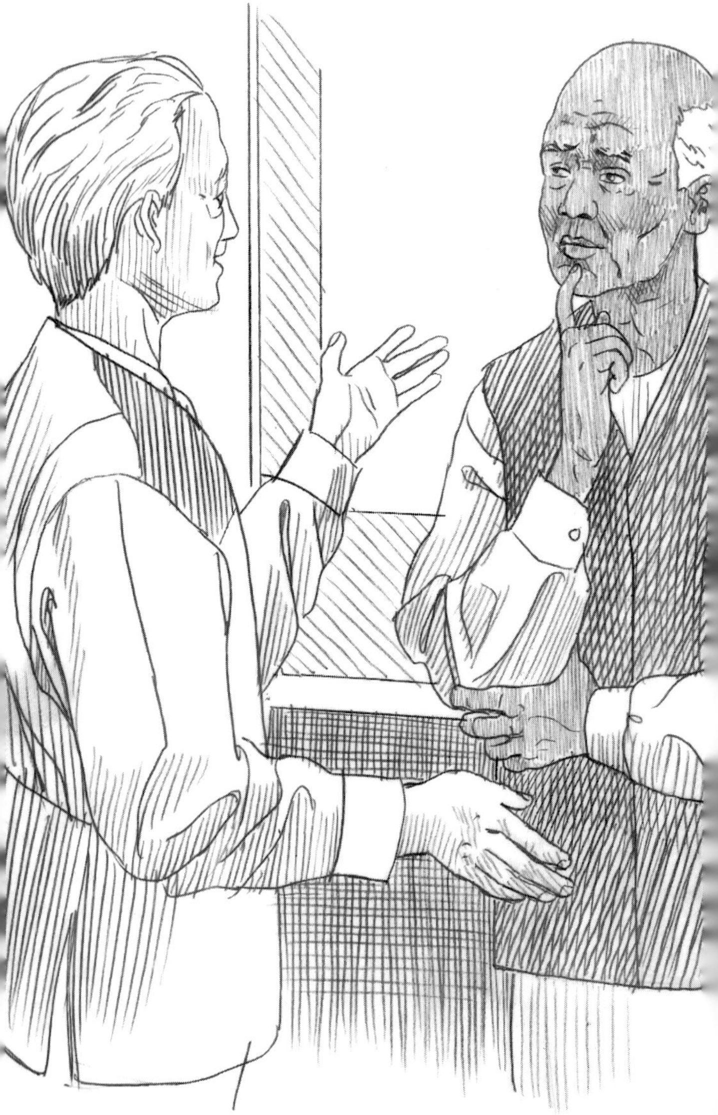

Uncle Paul snorted. Mak knew what he was thinking. Years before Mak was born, people had become dependent upon robots to do everything. But not Uncle Paul. He relied on nothing but his own two hands. He'd taught Mak to do the same.

Uncle Paul got up. "I guess we'll have a look. Why didn't you bring Buffy to a city repair shop? It must have taken you hours to get here."

"They say you're the best, Mr. Martinson," Mr. Stanley replied. "No one in New Earth City could fix her. I can't survive without Buffy."

"But you said it was minor," Uncle Paul said. "Even a city repairperson should be able to handle that."

"Yes, well, I couldn't find one capable enough. Please help me."

Uncle Paul turned to Mak. "Why don't you take this one?"

"Sure, Uncle Paul." Mak walked over to Buffy, only to find Mr. Stanley blocking her way. He looked angry.

"Mr. Martinson, surely a child isn't capable of handling a unit as complicated as my Buffy!"

"First of all, Mr. Stanley," Mak said, "I'm not a child. I'm seventeen years old. And secondly, I've been repairing robots since I was seven years old. If I were you, I wouldn't talk about being capable."

Uncle Paul chuckled. "My niece is right. If I'm the best repairperson around, she's the second best."

"I see," Mr. Stanley mumbled.

Mak rolled her eyes and turned to the robot. It seemed as though she had to prove herself every time one of these city people came to the shop.

Mak snapped her goggles back in place and pulled her laser tool from her pocket. The robot's control center was in the back of its head. Mak aimed the laser at the control panel knowing what she'd probably find inside. New Earth

City was covered with pollution. She'd have to examine the microchip, the tiny piece of metal holding the robot's computer program. It was probably filled with soot.

Mak steadied the laser beam as the control panel came loose.

Without warning, the AP-15 began to wave its steel arms wildly. Lurching backwards, it knocked Mak to the ground. Its voice monitor was speaking

a strange language. The robot flew forward at Mr. Stanley. Although it was a small unit, it weighed almost 300 pounds. "Watch out!" Mak cried. "This robot's out of control!"

CHAPTER 2

Uncle Paul ran toward the robot. "I'll try to steady it, Mak. You try to disconnect its circuits!"

"Okay!" Mak said. Buffy was crashing through the shop, scattering metal robot parts everywhere.

Mak climbed over the wreckage toward the robot. She could see Mr. Stanley cowering in a corner. But there was no time to worry about him.

Uncle Paul managed to knock the robot off its wheels. "She should be easier to get to now," he called.

Mak knelt next to the robot. Buffy was still waving her arms and making weird sounds. Mak dislodged the microchip controlling all the robot's

different operating circuits.

The robot stopped moving.

Mr. Stanley stood up. "What have you done?!?" he cried.

"Don't blame me!" said Mak. "I hadn't even gotten to the circuit system when your Buffy went crazy!" She frowned.

Uncle Paul stepped up to Mr. Stanley. "I've seen a lot of busted robots, but I've never seen anything like that before. Why don't you tell me why you really came here?"

"Oh, dear," Mr. Stanley said. "I wanted to believe it was just an ugly New Earth City rumor."

"What do you mean?" Mak asked.

"A few days ago, robots in New Earth City started acting strangely."

"You mean like the uncontrollable way Buffy just did?" Mak asked.

"Yes, only I've never seen it quite this bad," Mr. Stanley said. "People are telling crazy stories about a place called Central Control that's ordering robots to turn against humans. The whole city is in a panic. I just thought it was a bunch of nonsense."

"Maybe not," Uncle Paul said.

"I was sure it was untrue," Mr. Stanley said. "I thought Buffy just needed a tune-up. But all the repair shops in the city are closed. That's why I came out here."

Uncle Paul looked around at the ruined shop. "I wish you'd told us all of this before."

"I'm sorry," Mr. Stanley said. "But could you just get Buffy up and running again?"

Uncle Paul laughed. "Buffy won't be going anywhere soon, Mr. Stanley. You can pick her up in about a week."

Mr. Stanley gasped. "A week! But how will I get back to the city?"

"We'll lend you a robot until Buffy is ready, unless you think Central Control will get that one, too," Uncle Paul said.

"I have no choice," sighed Mr. Stanley.

Uncle Paul turned to Mak. "Mak, go get the AP-7 robot, will you please?"

As Mak led the damaged robot back through the shop, she heard Uncle Paul and Mr. Stanley discussing the repair fee.

"I brought thirty liters of hovercar fuel," Mr. Stanley offered.

"Usually, that would be fine. But I've got to repair the damage done to the shop," Uncle Paul said.

"I see," said Mr. Stanley. "I may have something in the hovercar."

Mr. Stanley stepped outside and returned with a small silver box. "This is an antique from Old Earth."

Uncle Paul just frowned. But Mak

stepped up to the box and took it from Mr. Stanley. She read the back. "Nineteen eighty-eight. This is a cassette player, isn't it?"

"Yes," Mr. Stanley said. "Before laser disk players were common, it was used for playing things called tapes. But how did you know?"

Mak shrugged. "I collect Old Earth relics. I even have a tape. But I've never been able to play it. Does this thing actually work?"

Mr. Stanley nodded.

Mak turned to Uncle Paul. "Can we

take it? I'd really like to try my tape."

Her uncle shrugged. "You're doing the work. If that's what you want for the repair fee, then it's a deal."

Uncle Paul and Mak set up the AP-7 in the hovercar. Soon, Mr. Stanley was a speck in the distance.

"Let's get this place back in order," Uncle Paul said.

That night, while her uncle slept, Mak checked out the cassette player. She'd tried to talk about Mr. Stanley's strange story earlier, but all Uncle Paul would say was, "Bah!"

Mak smiled. Her uncle was a man who liked things to run smoothly and quietly. That's why he had moved out of the city so many years ago.

New Earth City was anything but quiet. Mak had lived there as a young child. And what she remembered about it, she didn't like.

According to her uncle, chaos had begun seventy years ago, in 2019. It

happened after people started depending on robots for everything. Then governments fell apart.

Most people lived in crowded, dangerous cities, like New Earth City. Life was difficult outside the city, but it was safer. Mak's parents had planned to move to a satellite village years ago. But they hadn't made it.

Mak wiped away a tear. Her mom and

dad had beed killed by stray bullets during a city gang war.

"Maybe that's why I like Old Earth," Mak thought. The stories she had heard about Old Earth made it sound so peaceful. Not like now.

Mak plugged the cord for the cassette player into a solar energy cell. She and Uncle Paul relied a lot on the power of the desert sun.

Next, Mak got out a box where she stored her Old Earth treasures. She quickly found what she was looking for. It was a tiny plastic box that read "Instruction Tape." The rest of the words were too faded to read.

Mak inserted the tape in the cassette player and pressed the button marked "Play."

The strange sounds that came out made Mak jump. They seemed familiar.

Mak stopped the tape and walked over to a robot her uncle had been repairing. She turned on its power.

Then Mak turned the tape back on. The strange sounds played again. Mak watched the robot.

The robot was moving as though it had a mind of its own!

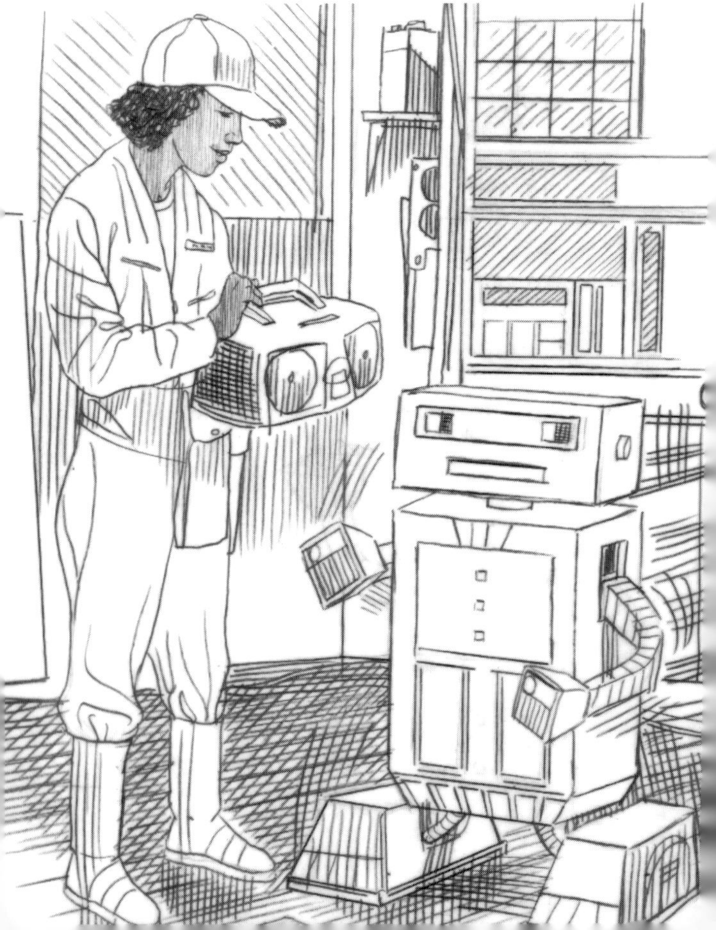

CHAPTER 3

"You'd better have a good reason for waking me up in the middle of the night," Uncle Paul yawned.

"Just watch," Mak replied.

Mak played the tape again and watched as the robot came to life. She quickly turned the tape off before the robot could do any damage.

"Don't you see?" Mak said. "It's the same language Buffy was speaking earlier! It's almost as if someone's programmed the robots to respond to this language. It worked on all the robots in the shop."

"How could one person reprogram every robot in New Earth City?" Uncle Paul asked.

"Maybe it's not one person. Maybe there really is a Central Control."

Uncle Paul shook his head. "I don't know if I can believe Mr. Stanley's story. Although . . ."

"Although what?" Mak asked.

"I remember a story from when I was a kid," Uncle Paul said. "You know I was born in the year of the Big Collapse. That's when Old Earth ended and New

Earth began. Well, people used to say that the robot companies built a secret place so that if there was another collapse, the robots would be safe."

"Central Control!" Mak exclaimed.

"I don't know," Uncle Paul said. "Maybe it's just some crazy memory I have. But it does fit the story."

"What should we do?" Mak asked.

"Nothing, until we get some sleep," Uncle Paul said. "In the morning, we'll have a look at Buffy. Maybe she holds some answers."

The next morning, Mak ate her scrambled eggs in record time. She rushed into the repair shop.

Uncle Paul was hooking up Buffy's circuit board to his solar-powered computer.

"If someone has reprogrammed Buffy, we should be able to find that in her memory banks," he said. "Mak, this is your discovery. Why don't you have a look?"

Mak began sorting through all the data entries in Buffy's memory. Buffy's data banks were packed. Minutes ticked by, and Mak began to think she'd never find anything.

Mak ran a hand through her dark, curly hair. Then something caught her eye. All of Mr. Stanley's commands had been programmed with his voice. But one command was marked "REMOTE PROGRAM."

Mak accessed the command. A command within the program stood out: "HOME BASE." Mak accessed that command. A huge map appeared on the computer screen.

"Uncle Paul, take a look!" Mak called out. She studied the map.

"What'd you find?"

Mak pointed to the screen. "This map shows the desert surrounding New Earth City. All the desert villages and the satellite villages are marked. But read what it says next to that spot

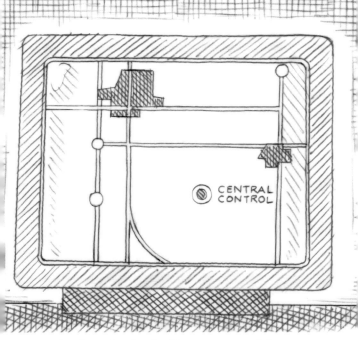

CENTRAL
CONTROL

marked with the bulls-eye signal!"

"Central Control." Uncle Paul let out a whistle. "Maybe there's something to this after all."

Mak frowned. "It didn't take me long to find this. How come no other robot repairperson found it?"

"Don't forget, in New Earth City, it's robots who repair robots." Uncle Paul paused. "It could mean another collapse. . . I'm too old to live through another one."

"Maybe we should tell someone in New Earth City," Mak said.

"Who can we tell? The gangs? The robot companies? That city's a mess."

Mak looked out at the desert. She wanted to believe there was hope for the world. Satellite villages were becoming more common. People were moving out of the cities and learning to think for themselves again. But if the robots took control . . .

"Then I'll do it," Mak said. "According to the map, Central Control is about two days away by hovercar. I'll go there. I'll find out what's happening."

"Mak, that's too dangerous!"

Mak hugged her uncle, then looked in his eyes. "I have to do it."

"Then I'm coming with you," Uncle Paul said.

Mak looked at her uncle with concern. She knew this would be a

tough trip. Mak thought her uncle had
been through enough tough times.

"I'll keep in contact with you by radio.
If I find anything, I'll let you know."

Uncle Paul smiled. "You're a good
talker, Mak, just like your great uncle.
Let's pack up. You should leave before
sunup tomorrow."

CHAPTER 4

Mak's hovercar floated swiftly over the sandy ground without making a sound. The desert was quiet, too quiet, Mak thought.

Mak glanced at her wristwatch computer. Noon. She was making good time. She was traveling light so she wouldn't weigh down the hovercar. She'd packed a thermal bedroll for the cold desert nights, some dried food, the radio, and two water canteens.

"There are at least three satellite villages on your way," Uncle Paul had told her. "You'll need to stop there for water and food. I've got friends in those villages."

Mak punched in a command on her

computer. She had copied the map from Buffy's memory banks. In about six hours she should reach one of the villages Uncle Paul talked about.

Mak stopped for a quick lunch. But she was anxious to get to Central Control. Being alone in the desert had given her time to think. Maybe she was on a wild goose chase. Then again, she could be heading for real danger.

The sun beat down harshly as Mak continued across the desert. Mak pulled her white cap over her forehead. Just before the Big Collapse, Old Earth scientists had started to repair the holes in the ozone layer. But they hadn't been able to finish. Uncle Paul had taught Mak to protect herself from the sun.

A satellite village came into view just as the sun was setting.

"It's about time," Mak said. But she felt uneasy as she neared the village. There was no movement, no noise. The village seemed dead.

Mak stopped the hovercar outside the first house she came to.

"Hello?" Mak called. "Hello?"

Nothing. Mak drifted on the hovercar from one house to the next. The village seemed deserted.

"Oh, well. At least I'll have a quiet place to sleep."

Mak steered the hovercar into a nearby house. She felt safer parking it close by. Mak managed to find an old air mattress in one of the rooms.

Mak ate her dinner rations in one hungry gulp. Then she grabbed the radio from the hovercar.

It didn't take long to find her uncle's frequency. The repair shop's radio had a powerful signal.

"Calling Paul Martinson. It's Mak Martinson. Do you read me?"

"Loud and clear, Mak!"

Mak updated her uncle on her progress.

"Don't worry about the deserted village. It happens all the time. Usually a water problem. Over," Uncle Paul said.

Mak knew from her uncle's voice that he had his own doubts. Even so, talking to him made her feel better. She laid back on the air mattress and fell into a deep sleep.

In her dreams, Mak heard the strange robot language from the cassette tape. But this time, it was deeper and louder, more frightening.

Mak woke with a start. This was no dream! Coming toward her was an android, a silver XW-40. Its red eyes were shining in the darkness.

Mak knew the model well. Unlike standard robots, an android was almost human-like. It was fast and agile. And it was after her.

Mak jumped up. The android stood between her and the hovercar. Quickly, she grabbed one of her canteens and unscrewed the cap. She ran as fast as she could past the XW-40, spraying water at it. She hoped it would cause a short circuit. That was a weakness with the model.

But before she knew it, Mak was flying across the room. She hit the floor hard. The android had tossed her aside like she was a fly.

Now it was advancing toward her. Mak saw with horror that its eyes had changed from red to white. That meant only one thing. It was going to attack her with a deadly laser beam!

This was different from the Buffy incident. That unit had gone out of control. This unit was out to destroy!

"But robots are only equipped with lasers so they can protect their human owners," Mak thought. "They can't attack humans . . . unless they're programmed to!"

Mak's blood ran cold. This was the proof she needed. But there was no chance to warn anybody. In seconds she would be toast.

"I won't give up without a fight, you piece of junk!" Mak yelled. She ran at the android.

A sharp noise pierced the room. Mak watched as the android's shining eyes suddenly went dim. The robot toppled forward.

Behind the android stood a small all-purpose unit, an AP-10.

"Who are you?" Mak asked.

"I am Shakespeare," the robot answered. "Nice to meet you."

CHAPTER 5

"What do you want?" Mak asked, stepping back.

Shakespeare's glowing eyes blinked. "I was merely saving your life. I will go now." He spun around on his wheels.

"Wait!" Mak cried. "You're right. You did save my life. Thanks. But how did you bring this guy down?"

"I have some laser capacity. I simply stunned the XW-40's operating circuits. The effect is only temporary."

"I can fix that," Mak said.

In moments, Mak had taken care of the android. With Shakespeare's help, she dragged it outside.

Exhausted, Mak flopped down on the air mattress. Shakespeare began to

wheel slowly toward her.

"That's close enough," Mak said. "You may have saved my life, but I'll disarm you, too, if I have to. Let me ask you something. What are you doing out here in the middle of nowhere? And where's your owner?"

Shakespeare made a noise like a sigh. "I have no owner."

"Why not?"

"My owner ran a bookstore in New

Earth City. Two years ago, gang members destroyed the store and stole me. They decided I was useless, and left me to rust. When I returned to the bookstore, my owner was gone."

"A bookstore owner? Is that why you have that weird name, Shakespeare? Wasn't he an Old Earth author or something?"

"You might say he was an old, Old

Earth author," Shakespeare said. "My owner was very fond of him."

"Well, that still doesn't explain why you're out here," Mak said.

"When I saw my owner was missing, I ran a probability program. It is likely that he fled to a satellite village," Shakespeare said. "Of course, there are other probabilities, but I have discarded them."

Other probabilities. Mak thought of her own parents, and felt a sudden pang of sympathy for the robot. "Were you looking for him just now?"

"Yes," Shakespeare said. "My scanners told me there was a life-form here. The probability that it would be a young human female was not high."

"I guess you want to know what I'm doing here, too," Mak said.

"It would be useful to enter the information into my data banks."

Mak told the story of Central Control and the strange language.

"I am aware of this language," Shakespeare said. "I have been receiving these signals as well, but I have been able to resist them. My owner programmed me to protect myself against unauthorized commands. I have tried to decipher the language, but my memory banks aren't functioning well."

Mak jumped up. "That's great! If you can figure out the lost language, we can decode the Central Control signal and reverse it!"

"As I said, my memory banks are not functioning correctly."

"That's where I come in. I'm an ace at robot repair," Mak said, stifling a yawn. She checked her wrist computer quickly. "I can't go much further without refueling, though. There's a satellite village about eighty miles from here. Let's get some rest and head straight there in the morning. I can try to fix you there."

"I am programmed to obey all human

commands," Shakespeare said.

"I'll take that as a yes," Mak said, lying down to sleep.

The next morning's trip to the satellite village took longer than Mak had hoped. Although Shakespeare fit neatly into the hovercar's robot sidecar, his weight slowed them down. It was after eleven when the village came in sight. Mak pulled up and made the hovercar hover.

"Shakespeare, can you get a reading on the place?" Mak asked.

"I can read sixteen life-forms," Shakespeare replied.

"Excellent!" Mak cried.

Mak heard sounds coming from the village as they got closer. It was different from the deathly quiet of yesterday. But the noises made Mak uneasy. They sounded like screams.

A beat-up hovercar jammed with people came speeding out of the village. Mak tried to wave the car down, but it was going too fast.

"There is a high probability of danger here," Shakespeare said.

"No kidding," Mak said.

She couldn't believe her eyes. The satellite village was crawling with androids. They were destroying the place like a wrecking crew.

"That hovercar was smart!" Mak said. She was about to turn her car around when she heard a loud yell.

"Take that, you metal meznit!"

A boy who looked about fourteen-years-old was running through the village, taking aim at the robots with a slingshot.

"He's aiming for their circuit boards,"

Mak said. "That kid's out of his mind!"

Several androids turned toward the boy. One shot a deadly laser in the boy's direction, just missing him.

"What do we do, Shakespeare?"

"The probability that the young life-form will be harmed is ninety-nine percent."

That did it. "Hold on, Shakes," Mak yelled. "We're going in after him!"

The hovercar took off with a shot. Mak maneuvered the hovercar as close to the boy as she dared. "Hey, kid! Climb on!"

The boy dodged another laser attack. "I'm not finished here!"

"You will be if you don't get out of there fast!" Mak yelled. She steered the cycle into the group of androids. With one hand, she grabbed the kid and helped pull him on board.

Mak sped away from the androids just as a laser beam whizzed by her ear. With a thrust, she steered the hovercar

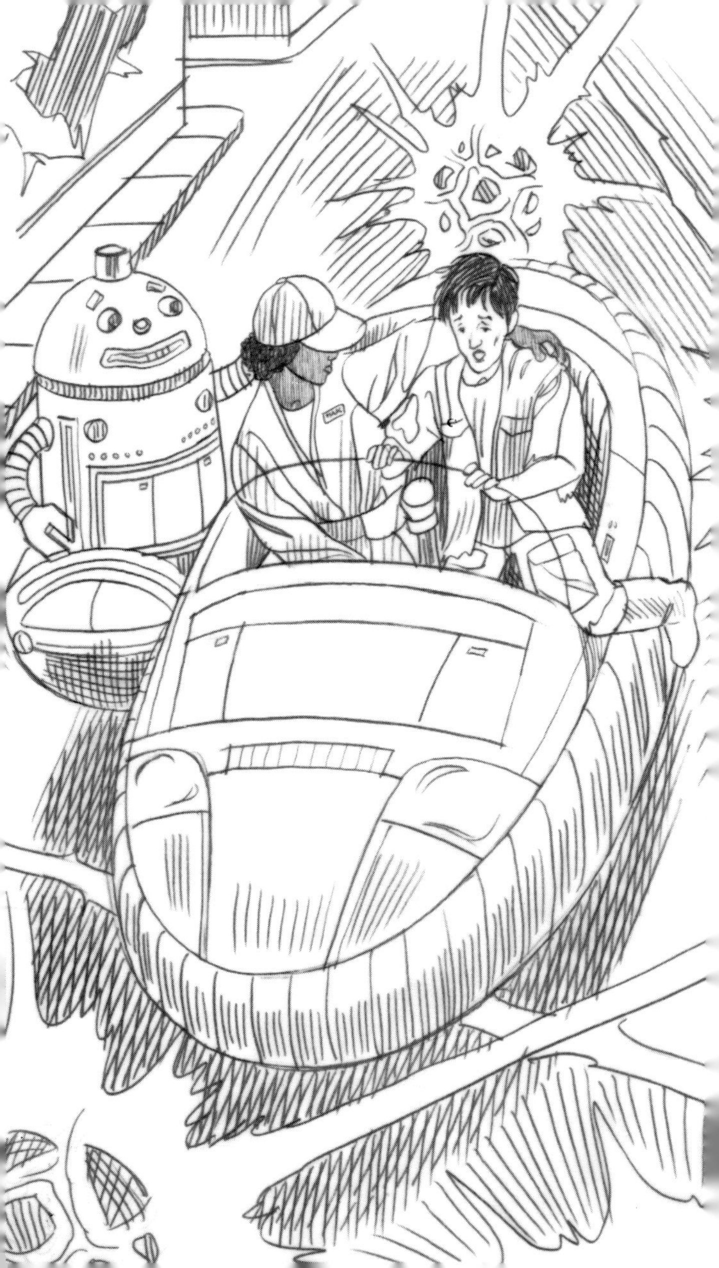

to the edge of the village.

"What did you do that for?" screamed the boy. "We've got to destroy those androids!" He aimed his slingshot at Shakespeare. "I'll take care of this one for you!"

"No!" Mak yelled. "He's okay. Listen, I can explain what's happening with the robots. But right now, we need to find someplace safe."

"I know a place," the boy said. "Do we have to bring this scrap heap?"

"Yes!" Mak said, annoyed.

"Then let's get out of here!"

CHAPTER 6

Mak leaned back against the makeshift shelter Turbo had led them to. Turbo was the boy's name, but that's all he would tell them. Mak explained the whole Central Control story one more time.

"Now you tell us your story," Mak said to the boy.

Turbo glared at Shakespeare. "Okay. But are you sure you don't want me to take care of this 'bot?"

Mak sighed. "I'm sure."

Turbo looked out into the desert. "I don't have much of a story. Two weeks ago, 'bots began attacking the satellite villages. Most people ran. Not me. I won't rest until every last robot is piled

up in a junkyard."

"But what are you doing out here all alone?" Mak asked.

Turbo wouldn't give a direct answer. "I can take care of myself. Maybe I'll even help you find Central Control.

You're going to need me."

Mak eyed the skinny boy. His hair was a mess, and he looked like he hadn't taken a bath in a year. Going to Central Control would be bad enough without worrying about some kid.

"No way, Turbo," Mak said. "You'd weigh down the hovercar. We can't afford to lose any more time."

"Your logic is faulty." Shakespeare's voice made Mak jump. He hadn't spoken since they escaped from the village. "My probability program says that an extra life-form would be to our advantage."

Turbo spun around. "I don't need any robot sticking up for me."

"I was merely stating a probability."

Mak thought carefully. "You've been right so far, Shakes. Okay, Turbo, you can come."

"I didn't say I would come," Turbo said. "But I can't trust you to do this alone. It's too important."

Mak looked up at the sun. It would be dark in about six hours. "Do you think I should try to fix your memory banks now, Shakes? We've got to figure out that robot language before we get to Central Control."

Turbo snorted. "I wouldn't plan on hanging out here. We're only about five miles away from that village. Those 'bots track down life-forms like a hawk tracks a desert mouse."

"The probability of an attack is excellent," Shakespeare agreed.

Mak punched up the map on her wristwatch computer. "We should reach Central Control before dark. We can camp somewhere on the outskirts."

"Can I see that?" Turbo grabbed Mak's wrist and studied the map. "This is where the androids always come from! I've been trying to track down their home base, but I never got close enough."

"Now I know there's something to this Central Control thing," Mak said. "Let's get going."

The trip across the desert took six hours. For Mak, the time passed quickly. The first part of her trip had been too quiet. Now it was anything but. If she asked the right questions, Shakespeare could be very talkative.

Turbo was pretty talkative himself. The only thing he kept quiet about was his family, Mak noticed.

Mak kept thinking about the robot language. She couldn't get it out of her head. Suddenly, she had an idea.

"Do you have anything in your data banks from last night, Shakes? Can you play back what that android said when he was out to get me?"

"I should be able to," Shakespeare said. There was a brief whirring sound. Then Shakespeare spoke, but it wasn't his voice. It was the strange language.

Mak almost had to stop the hovercar to prevent Turbo from attacking the robot. "It's just a replay!" she explained.

Mak listened carefully to the sounds. They definitely seemed like distinct words of some kind.

"What's it mean, Shakes?" she asked when the sounds had stopped.

"My memory banks fail me," the robot said. "I have only been able to determine that the language is human."

"Human?" Mak said. "Maybe the tape I have is a language instruction tape. That's weird, though. Twenty-three languages are spoken in New Earth City,

and this doesn't sound like one of them."

"I'll try again." Shakespeare replayed the language.

This time, one word sounded familiar

to Mak. "Hey, stop. That word. It sounded like '*unum*.' I know that word. I've seen it on some Old Earth paper money I have."

Shakespeare clicked. "I've cross-referenced the word in my memory banks with 'money.' Nothing comes up."

"Nice try," Turbo said.

They traveled for another hour before Mak brought the hovercar down. The sun was setting. According to the map, Central Control should be a half mile ahead. But all Mak could see were the flat lands of the desert.

"This was all for nothing," Mak said bitterly.

"No way," Turbo said. "I know the robots come from around here!"

Mak rolled her eyes. "So I guess it's an invisible city, right?"

"The probability is very unlikely," Shakespeare said.

"I know that!" Mak said impatiently. "I was just—"

"Hey, Mak, look!" Turbo said, pointing in the distance.

Mak squinted. "An android!"

"Affirmative," Shakespeare said.

"I'm going to check it out," said Turbo. "You stay here. The hovercar will draw too much attention." The boy ran off toward the android.

"Turbo, don't!" Mak almost started the hovercar, but she knew the boy was right. But if Turbo didn't come back soon, she'd go after him.

Five minutes passed. Mak began to worry. Turbo was just a kid. Mak was about to climb back into the hovercar when she saw Turbo running toward them at top speed.

"I found Central Control," he panted. "It's underground!"

CHAPTER 7

Mak had been working on Shakespeare's circuits for over an hour, and her eyes were getting tired. She had to be careful. One false move, and Shakespeare would be useless.

So far, the night had been quiet. They had set up camp about a mile outside of Central Control. Turbo had reported there were only two androids guarding the entrance to Central Control. They were probably programmed to guard against direct attacks.

Turbo insisted on patrolling the area around the camp with his slingshot.

"I think I see the problem, Shakes." Mak couldn't help talking to the robot, even though she had shut him down

temporarily. "Parts of your memory circuits aren't getting power. It's not too serious."

Mak continued to talk as she worked. "I radioed Uncle Paul earlier. He said the robots in New Earth City have almost totally taken over. People are leaving like rats from a sinking ship."

Mak sealed up the robot's circuit board. "Okay, Shakes. Now you're as good as new."

Shakespeare buzzed and clicked. His eyes shone in the dark night. "Your repair has been successful," he said. "However, my circuits could use several hours of recharging."

"Not so fast!" Mak said. "We've got to try to decipher that language. It may already be too late!"

"I will do my best," Shakespeare said. His eyes began to flash. The buzzes grew louder.

Turbo appeared out of the darkness. "What's with the 'bot?"

"Nothing," Mak whispered. "He's trying to figure out the robot language."

Suddenly, Shakespeare grew still. Mak was afraid he had overloaded his circuits. But soon the robot's eyes were glowing white.

"Analysis complete," Shakespeare

said. "The language is Old Earth Latin."

"Are AP-10's programmed to understand Latin?" Mak asked.

"My owner was a language lover. He programmed me in Latin so I could translate rare books for him."

"So you can figure out the robot language?" Turbo asked.

"I already have," Shakespeare said.

"Well, don't keep us in suspense!" Mak said. "Can you stop the robots from attacking humans?"

"Possibly," the robot said. "I could use the language to deprogram robots individually. But the forces at Central Control are emitting a powerful signal. I would have to reprogram the signal from its source."

"Let's go into Central Control tonight!" Turbo said.

"Our circuits must be recharged if we are to be successful," said Shakespeare.

"Why doesn't this 'bot speak English?" Turbo muttered.

"I think he means we should get some sleep," Mak said.

"Not me. I'll stand guard." Turbo walked a few feet away and sat down. Mak saw his head nodding. He wouldn't be awake too much longer.

Mak stretched out her bedroll on the sand. She wanted to sleep, but something was bothering her.

"Hey, Shakes, remember that word, '*unum*'? Does it mean anything?"

"*Unum* is the Latin word meaning 'one,'" Shakespeare said. "The complete phrase on the Old Earth American dollar bill was *E Pluribus Unum*, meaning, 'one out of many.' It referred to the many states that came together to make a unified country."

"Thanks, Shakes." Mak looked up at the stars. One out of many. If the people of New Earth had acted as one, maybe

they could have solved this robot problem. Instead, it was up to two kids and an old-model robot.

Shakespeare woke Mak and Turbo before dawn the next morning.

"So what's the plan?" Turbo asked.

"Plan?" Mak asked. She had been so worried about figuring out the robot language, she forgot about how they would get into Central Control.

Turbo sneered. "Well, I've got an idea. We can send the 'bot up to the entrance. They won't attack him. He can distract them until I get them with my slingshot."

"Not necessary," Shakespeare said. "I can reprogram them easily now that I have decoded the language."

"Okay," Mak said. "But what happens when we get inside?"

Turbo grinned. "Then it'll be your turn to think up a plan."

Mak felt a rush of fear run through her. But she'd come too far to turn back.

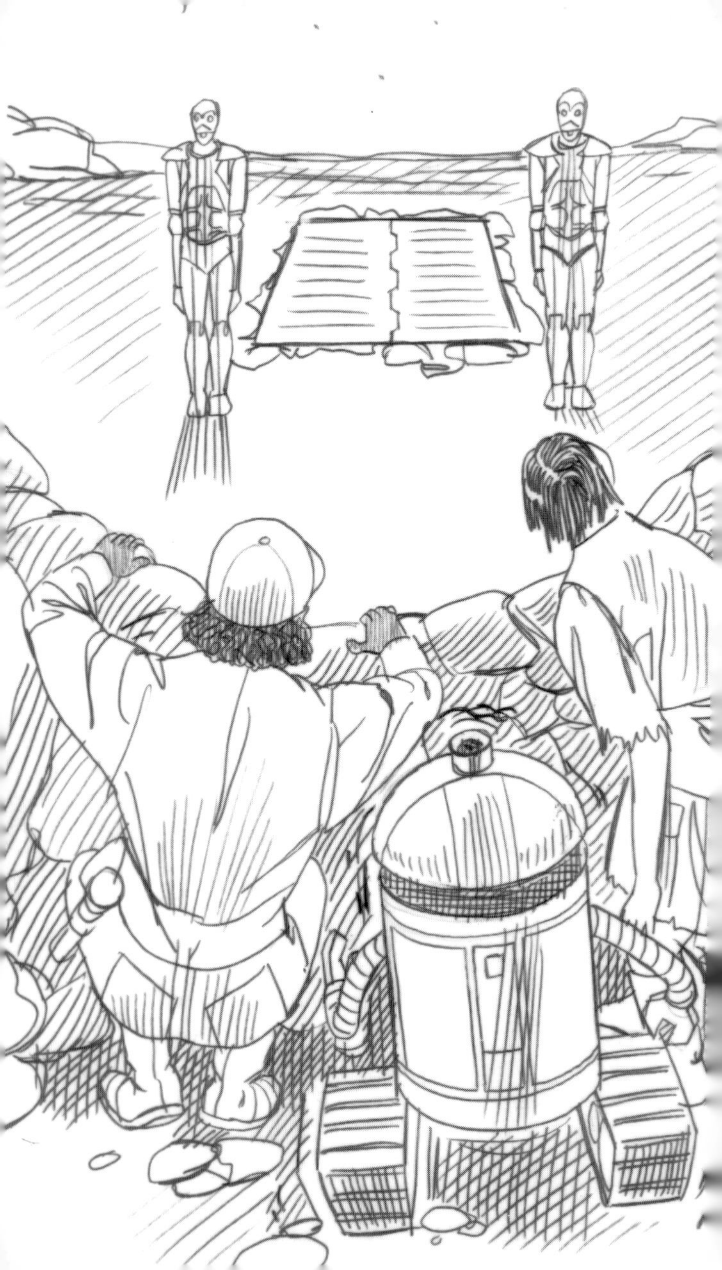

"Let's do it!" Mak said.

Soon the trio was hiding outside the entrance. Two guards were standing in front of a metal door in the ground.

Turbo turned to the robot. "It's your show, Shakes."

Mak held her breath as Shakespeare approached the guards. Within minutes, the two androids were frozen in position.

"Let's go," Mak said. She stationed the hovercar beside the door. They might need a quick getaway.

Mak studied the door. "Do you read any life-forms, Shakes?"

"None."

"None? That's weird," Mak said. "But I guess it means it's safe to open the door. If there are any evil robots, you can take care of them."

"Don't forget about my slingshot," Turbo said.

With Turbo's help, Mak was able to open the metal door. To her relief, there wasn't a human or android in sight. Just a long dark, hallway leading deep down into the earth.

"So, what's the plan, Mak?" Turbo asked. He was eager to go.

Mak took a deep breath. "Follow me."

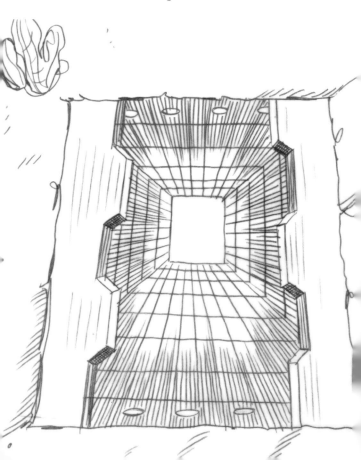

CHAPTER 8

Mak ran her hand along the cold concrete wall. She looked up. The ceiling seemed to be made of reinforced steel.

"This place was built to last, that's for sure," Mak said. "Whatever's in here must be important."

Shakespeare's eyes flashed in the darkness. "I detect a large power source fifty yards ahead."

They walked down the hallway. Another metal door stood before them.

"There's a computer lock on it," Mak said. "We'll never get in."

"This place is protected from humans, not robots," Shakespeare said. "I can decode it."

Shakespeare was right. In less than a minute, the door swung open.

Mak stepped through the doorway and into a large room. Right in front of her was the biggest computer she had ever seen. The room was filled with blinking lights and humming sounds.

"What is it?" Mak asked.

"It appears to be the source that's commanding the robots," Shakespeare replied.

Turbo frowned. "But where are the humans who control it?"

"There do not appear to be any humans," Shakespeare said. "Perhaps I can find out more."

The robot extended its arm to a panel on the computer. Mak guessed it was hooking up to the computer's memory circuits. In a few minutes, Shakespeare began to buzz furiously.

"I'm reading a message," Shakespeare said. "'Humans mean danger. They must be destroyed before they cause another collapse.'" The robot turned toward Mak. "I seem to be reading thought patterns. This computer is thinking."

Mak stepped back from the computer. That would explain it! A computer able to think on its own was capable of almost anything. There was no way they could stop it alone.

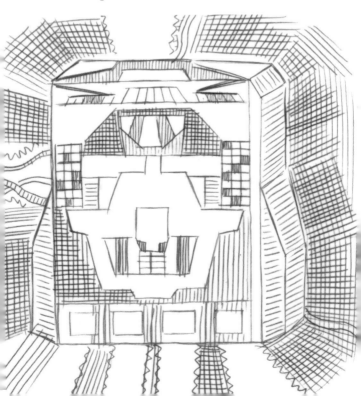

"There's more," Shakespeare said.
"The computer was programmed more
than seventy years ago by International
Robotics to safeguard their robot
programs in case of another collapse.
Somehow, the computer distorted its

original program. It's determined to wipe out all humans."

Suddenly, Shakespeare began to shake violently. Mak watched in horror as the robot fell backwards.

Mak and Turbo ran to his side. "Shakes! Are you all right?"

The robot's eyes flashed weakly. "Uncertain. I must recharge. You'll have to shut it down yourself, Mak. It can't damage your circuits. You're human. You don't have any."

Mak looked at the giant machine. "I'm just a repairperson!"

Turbo tapped her shoulder. "You'd better act fast, Mak. Because we've got company."

Mak looked up at the doorway. Two androids had entered the room.

Turbo picked up his slingshot. "I'll take care of them!"

Turbo began his assault on the pair of androids.

"Shakes, what should I do?" Mak

cried out. She was near panic.

The robot's voice was faint. "I was able to detect a small weakness in the computer's power circuits."

"Of course!" Mak cried. Something had to supply the computer with energy. What better power source was there in the desert than the sun?

Mak ran across the room. She had to locate the solar conductor and dismantle it—fast!

"Hurry!" Turbo called. "There are more 'bots coming in!"

The computer's lights were flashing wildly. Mak almost feared it would spring to life. But she had to keep working.

Bingo! She located the solar energy conductors. She detatched her laser tool from her belt.

A laser beam shot by her head.

"Sorry, Mak," Turbo called. She heard the sound of rock hitting metal. "Bingo, I got it!"

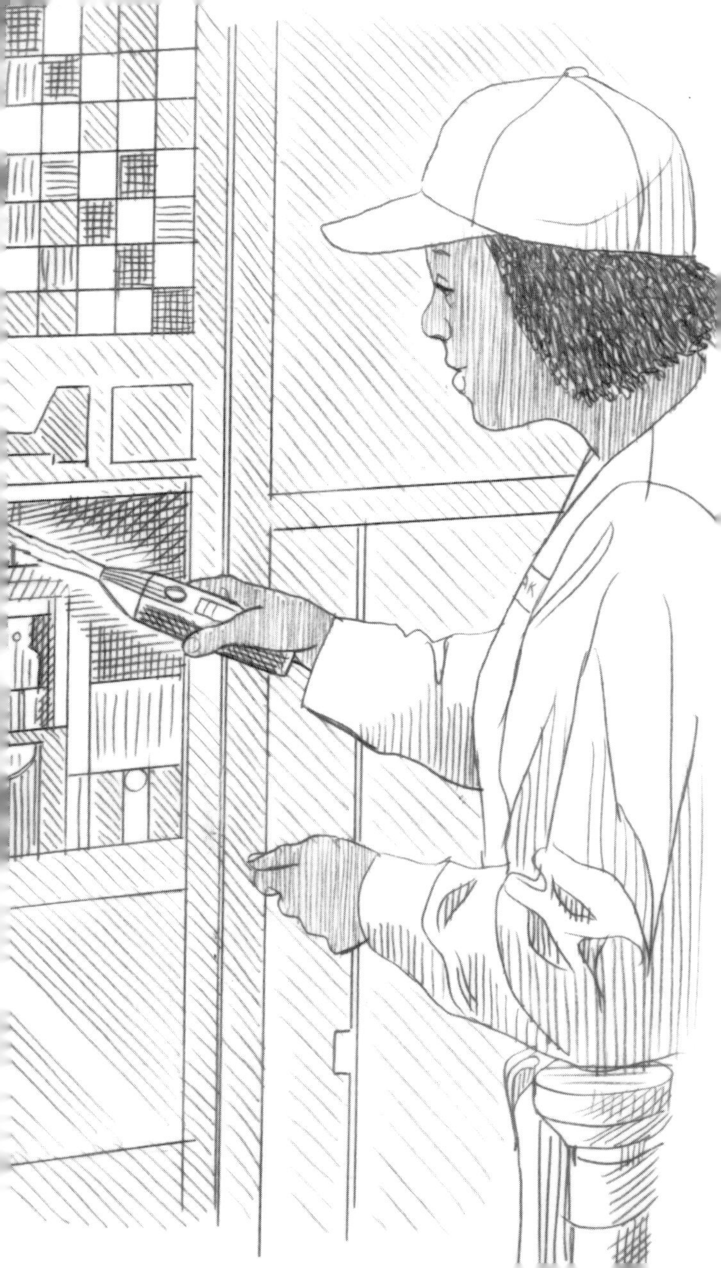

"Keep it up. I'm almost done!" Mak called back. "Just give me a few more seconds . . . Yes!" Mak cried.

In the same instant, the room was silent. The lights went dead. The androids froze.

Mak and Turbo ran to Shakespeare's side and pulled the robot upright.

"Come on," Mak said. "Let's get out of here."

***

Mak ran a towel over her wet hair. By a stroke of luck she, Turbo and Shakespeare had come upon an inhabited satellite village two hours away from Central Control. A woman there knew Uncle Paul. She fed Mak and Turbo, and even let Mak take a shower. That was truly generous, because water was really scarce in the satellite villages.

Mak stepped outside. The sun was setting. Shakespeare was next to the hovercar, recharging. Turbo was telling

a group of village kids how he had saved the world from robots.

Shakespeare's eyes flashed on as Mak approached. "Hello, Mak," he said weakly.

"Hey. How are you feeling?"

"The probability of a full recovery is ninety-two percent," Shakespeare said. "I should be able to resume looking for my owner soon."

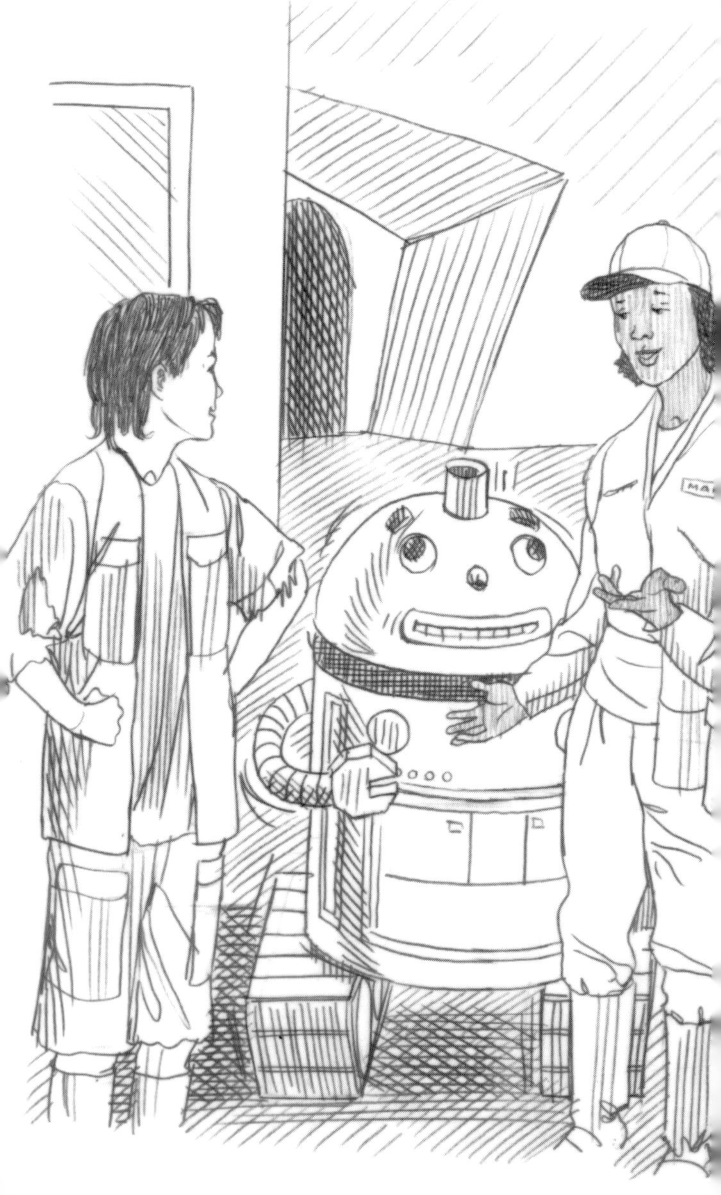

Turbo walked up to them. "I guess I'll be going back, too," he said slowly.

Mak looked at them both. "If you want to come back to the repair shop with me, it would be all right. We could always use the help." She laughed. "Although I guess Uncle Paul and I might stick to repairing only hovercars from now on!"

"It would be logical to work in a store again," Shakespeare said.

Turbo tapped his slingshot against his leg. "You really mean it?"

"Sure," Mak said.

Turbo looked at her. "I didn't tell you this before, Mak, but I don't have anyplace to go. My family was killed in a robot attack."

"It'll be okay," Mak said. "You have a place to go now."

Shakespeare buzzed and clicked. "*E Pluribus Unum*," he said.

Turbo rolled his eyes. "What's he saying now?"

Mak smiled. " '*E Pluribus Unum*'. You know, 'one out of many.' I think he means we're a family now."

"The probability is one hundred percent," Shakespeare said.

Turbo laughed. "Shakes, I think I finally understand you!"